P9-BYA-298

My
UNDEAD
LIFE

LOL
OMG
2+2
OMG
BRAINZ
LY2
LOL
2+2

OMG, ZOMBIE!

by Emma T. Graves

illustrated by Binny Boo

STONE ARCH BOOKS
a capstone imprint

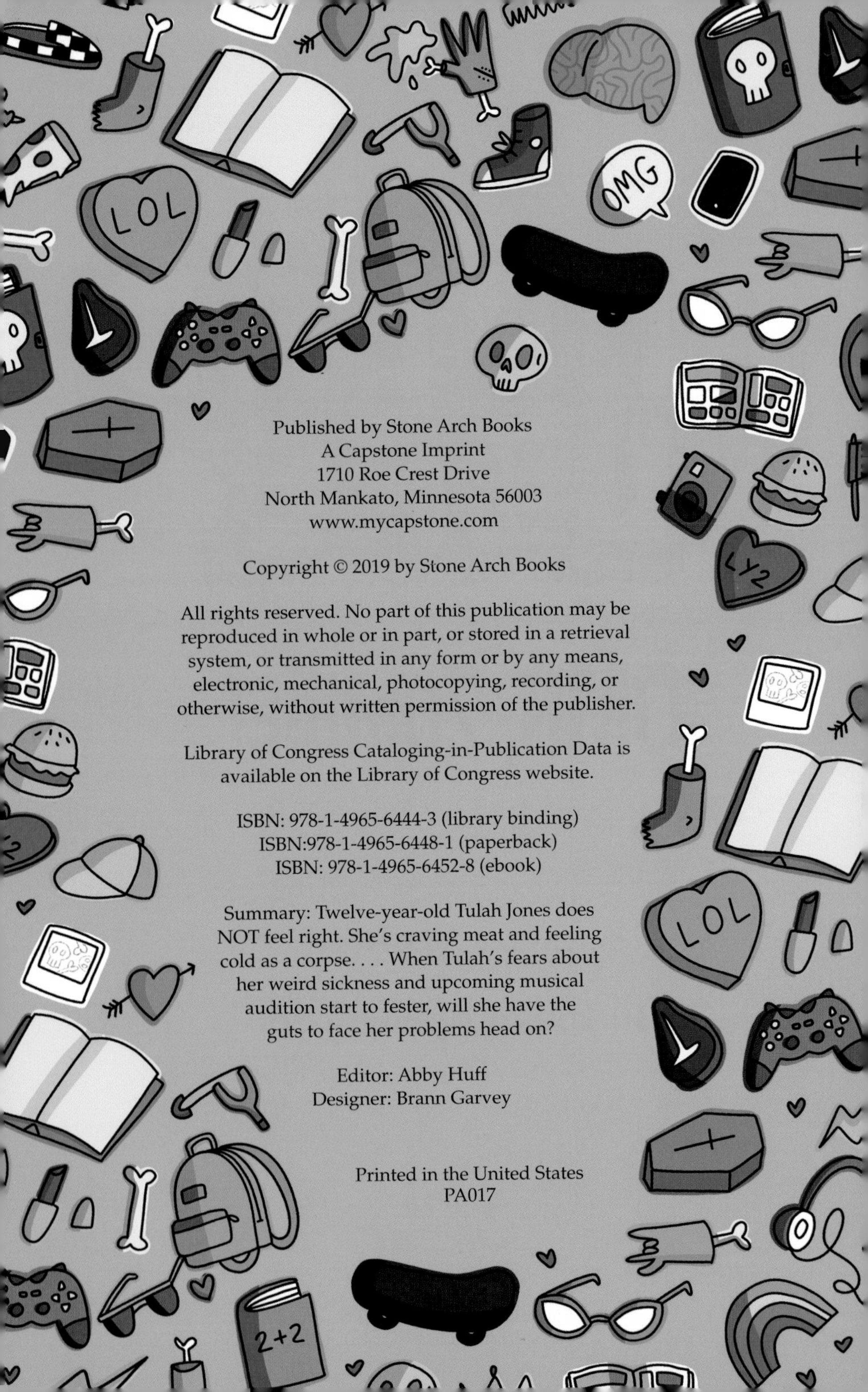

Published by Stone Arch Books
A Capstone Imprint
1710 Roe Crest Drive
North Mankato, Minnesota 56003
www.mycapstone.com

Library of Congress Cataloging-in-Publication Data is available on the Library of Congress website.

ISBN: 978-1-4965-6444-3 (library binding)
ISBN:978-1-4965-6448-1 (paperback)
ISBN: 978-1-4965-6452-8 (ebook)

Summary: Twelve-year-old Tulah Jones does NOT feel right. She's craving meat and feeling cold as a corpse. . . . When Tulah's fears about her weird sickness and upcoming musical audition start to fester, will she have the guts to face her problems head on?

Editor: Abby Huff
Designer: Brann Garvey

Printed in the United States
PA017

WARNING!
CAUTION!
BEWARE!

This story has some seriously creepy stuff. Including:

- Barfing
- School musical auditions (EEK!)
- Freaking out in front of secret crushes
- Mysterious urges to eat raw meat
- Ignoring your problems until the very last possible moment
- Annoying little brothers
- Oh yeah, and ZOMBIES

Keep reading if you want, but don't say I didn't warn you.

Hi! I'm Tulah Jones. I'm twelve years old, and I've just started at Evansville Middle School. I hope I can survive it!
My BFF, Nikki Corvos. We've been inseparable since kindergarten. She's loud and funny and does not have a shy bone in her body (the opposite of me).

My mom. She's a lawyer, which means she's great at arguing and likes to win. Ever try to convince a lawyer to let you have dessert before supper? Never gonna happen.

My dad. He's an accountant and big into sports. (He helps coach Jaybee's soccer team and the middle school cross-country team.) He also loves cheesy sayings that I call dadisms.

My little brother, Jaybee. He's totally dorky and totally annoying. He owns more zombie comics and books than any other 4th grader, or maybe even any library.

My biology lab partner, Angela Stone. Her family owns a funeral home, so she's always around dead people. Some kids say she's weird, but I think she's OK.

My crush, Jeremy Romero! Isn't he adorable?! He just started going to my school. Too bad I don't have the guts to talk to him.

LOL
OMG
2+2
LY2
BRAINZ
LOL
RIP
OMG
2+2

Have you ever been so sick you wanted to die?

I have, and let me tell you, it was the opposite of fun.

Seriously, I spent the last two days barfing my guts out. Two. Whole. Days. All the guts!

While I clung to the toilet bowl for dear life on Sunday night, I had plenty of time to think about my situation. What in the world had I done to deserve this sick fate?

Actually, I was pretty sure I already knew.

The reason I felt like death warmed over had everything to do with my lunch choice last Friday. Or rather, my *lack* of choice.

Last Friday . . .
I had come late to lunch on Mystery Meal day. A serious mistake for a vegetarian like me.
You see, all the clever omnivores had already snatched up the less disgusting plant-based option.
Meat
Meatless

Excuse me, do you have any more vegetarian meals?
Hmph. I'll look in the back.
PLOP!
BLURRRP
CREEEEK
The sounds coming from the kitchen weren't encouraging. And the cafeteria worker took forever, which was not a good sign.

SPLAT!
What she finally came up with barely looked like food.
I never should have eaten it.

I should've realized consuming whatever they'd managed to scare up from the depths of the cafeteria freezer would have consequences. But I was starving and desperate. That was what I got for skipping breakfast, "The most important meal of the day," as my dad would say.

So I made a grave mistake. I held my nose and wolfed down the "food" without asking questions.

But now, after spending forty-eight hours in the bathroom, I was full of questions. Like:

1. Why can't I get off this tile floor?
2. Will I ever want to eat again?
3. When did I put something *that* color in my mouth?
4. When am I going to feel normal?
5. Will I have an extreme fear of hot lunches for the rest of my life?

Cautiously, I pulled myself away from the toilet. I was almost positive it was impossible to throw up anything else. I crawled across the hall to my room and climbed into bed. I lay there feeling empty and lifeless.

My phone lit up beside me. It was a text from Nikki.

Nikki was my best friend. She was really funny. Most of the time.

NIKKI: *Hey, barf bag!*

ME: *Hey. :(*

NIKKI: *Your mom said you've been super sick. Still losing your lunch?*

NIKKI: *Driving the porcelain bus?*

NIKKI: *Checking in at the vomitorium?*

NIKKI: *Tossing your cookies?*

NIKKI: *Blowing chunks?*

ME: *NOT funny.* :'(

NIKKI: *Sorry. Srsly. Feeling any better?*

ME: *Not exactly better. Let's just say much, much emptier.*

NIKKI: *Empty is good. Don't want you puking on me at auditions on Thursday!* :P

Why did she have to mention *auditions*? Just when I thought I couldn't feel any worse!

I rolled over and closed my eyes. Now I *really* wished I was dead.

TWEEDLE TWEET! TWEEDLE TWEET!

My eyes suddenly flew open. A flock of birds were giving a recital right outside my window—and interrupting my slumber.

"UUUUGGGHHH," I groaned, burying my face in my pillow.

The birds' cheery song did nothing to brighten my mood. It just reminded me that I'd have to perform my own song soon.

Because on Thursday, I would be auditioning for the Evansville Middle School fall musical.

I peeked over at the sheet music on my desk.

"*Uuuuggghhh,*" I groaned again and shut my eyes.

To some people, auditioning might not seem like a big deal. But to me it was. To me it was a VERY big deal.

Now, don't get me wrong. I love musicals. I opened my eyes and stared at the ceiling. The amazing composer and actor Lin Manuel Miranda stared back at me from the *Hamilton* poster hanging over my bed. He was giving me a small smile, like he *knew* that I knew every word of his musical (and countless others).

"Yes!" I sighed, annoyed.

Lin was right. I did love singing and dancing! I did love the stage! I just *hated* being on it.

The first and last time I stepped onto the stage had been a major disaster. It was back in first grade. Our class had learned to play the bells for the holiday show. I had been so excited to show off my jingle-bell skills. We had all filed out, each of us wearing a matching elf hat.

Then, on cue, we turned and faced the audience.

That was when I froze. My whole body locked up and shut down and . . .

I did a full face-plant right in front of everyone.

Yes, I had fainted. Yes, I was that lame. I had to be carried off the stage with a bloody nose.

Since then I knew I could never be a leading star. Not with my nerves. So I've always stuck with behind-the-scenes jobs for school plays and musicals. I've become an expert at holding back curtains.

TBH, I would've been happy working backstage forever. But my friend Nikki had other plans. She was determined to drag me out into the spotlight with her. Which is why my best friend decided to trick me.

It all started with a game of Truth or Dare at Lacey DuChamp's sleepover the weekend before.

"Your turn, Tulah!" Lacey had shouted. "What'll it be, truth or dare?"

"Dare," I had answered immediately.

I didn't often go in for the dare. But I couldn't pick truth this time. Not with Bella Gulosi using all the truth questions to find out who liked the new boy at Evansville, Jeremy Romero.

Because I totally *did* like Jeremy Romero, and I totally *didn't* want Bella to know.

You see, Bella was my worst enemy. Ever since I beat her in the fourth-grade spelling bee, she had been working to make my life miserable. Letting my nemesis know the name of my crush would only lead to disaster.

So, dare it was.

Tulah Jones, I dare you to eat canned dog food.
I really didn't think there could be a worse dare than Bella's.

No! I dare you to try out for *Musical High!*
I was wrong.
Ooh, yeah. Perfect!
Bella must've seen the fear all over my face.
Uh, it's OK. I can eat the dog food.
Nope! It's decided. You're trying out!

I had pleaded with Nikki with my eyes, but my BFF just grinned.

"Trust me," she had whispered in my ear. "You can beat your stage fright if you just face it head on! This is for your own good."

I hated when people said that. Rarely did it actually lead to anything good.

All I could do was scream silently in my head. We performed a quick pinky swearing ceremony to make sure that I wouldn't chicken out.

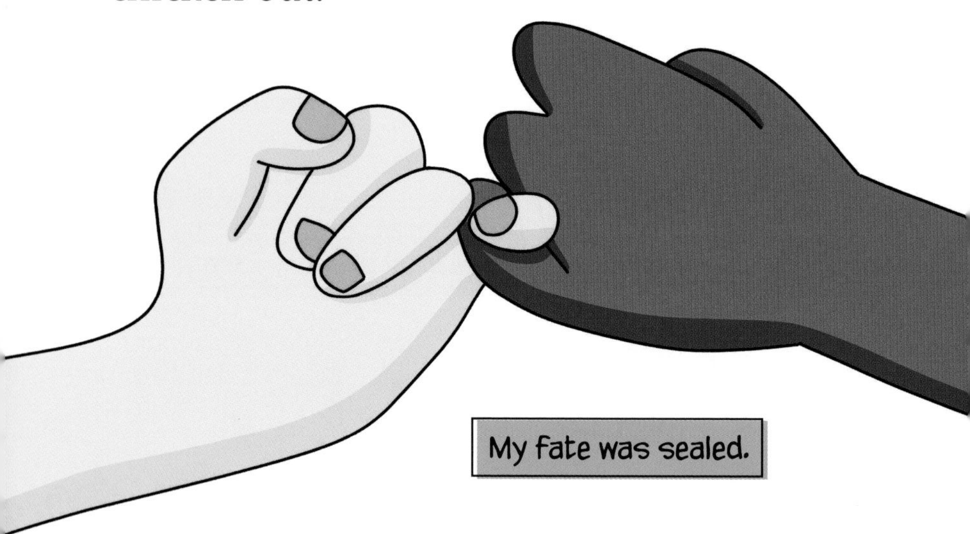

Ugh. Remembering the pinky swear made me wish I had never woken up.

I picked up my phone to distract my brain. When I looked at the screen, my eyes nearly popped out of my skull. I had twelve unread texts! They were all from Nikki.

But what was really making my eyes bug out was the date stamp.

Tuesday, 4:35 p.m.

I'd been asleep for more than twenty-four hours! I'd missed two days of school! And auditions were even sooner than I thought!

I scrolled through Nikki's texts.

NIKKI: *Hello?*

NIKKI: *Are you there?*

NIKKI: *Tulah, did you die or something?*

NIKKI: *You're freaking me out!*

NIKKI: *If this is about auditions . . .*

But it was Nikki's last text that sent a shiver down my spine.

NIKKI: *Tulah? SRSLY, I hope you're OK! But don't think for a minute you're getting out of auditions. I'll drag you onto the stage myself if I have to. :)*

I pulled my covers over my head. My life was over! Or maybe I just wished it was.

DING-A-LING DING-A-LING!

I guess I had fallen back asleep, because I woke up to my school alarm chiming from my phone the next morning. I automatically pulled myself to sitting, then fell out of bed.

Like, for real. I hit the floor with a *THUD.*

"Ow," I mumbled. Apparently I'd been sick for so long I had forgotten how to stand.

"Let's go, legs!" I said, hoping a little encouragement would get my stubborn limbs moving.

It kind of helped. I lurched forward. There were a few close calls going down the stairs, but I made it into the kitchen without wiping out.

My parents were already there, dressed for work, drinking coffee, and checking their phones. They both had pretty high-powered jobs. Mom was a lawyer, and Dad managed an accounting firm (plus coached soccer and cross-country on the side). Work always started before they made it to the office.

My little fourth-grade brother, Jaybee, was working too. He was busy shoveling a bowl of Peanut-Choco Explosion cereal into his face.

But everyone stopped and stared at me as soon as I stumbled in. It was as if they'd just seen a ghost.

"It's alive!" Jaybee hooted between a full mouth of his extra-sugary breakfast. He was quoting his favorite movie, *Frankenstein*.

"Ha, ha. Very funny," I said. Jaybee thought he was hilarious. I thought he was a pain. "I was sick, not dead!"

"Oh, honey, I'm so glad you're up! I was just about to call Dr. Phranc again," Mom said, putting down her phone. She came over and examined my face. "I tried to wake you last night to give you a sip of water. But it was impossible! You were out cold. How are you feeling now?"

"Pretty good, actually," I replied.

That was the truth. I felt weirdly OK for a person who had been yakking up their guts for two days and then sleeping it off for two more. I should've been sore or weak or something. But aside from being a little stiff, I felt fine.

"Can I get you anything for breakfast?" Mom asked.

"Um . . . ," I started.

I looked at Mom's smoothie. I looked at Dad's fried egg sandwich. I looked at Jaybee's cereal. None of it looked good. It was Wednesday morning, and I hadn't eaten since last Friday. I should've been starving, but I wasn't hungry at all.

"No, that's all right," I said. "I'll just have something small."

I grabbed a banana from the fruit bowl.

Herk-
BLEGH!
Ah,
gross!

Heh. I guess I don't have my appetite back yet.
NEWS

I could not get that banana out of my mouth fast enough. It did NOT taste like banana. That was slimy, squishy dirt.

I handed the rest of the evil banana to my dad. He thought it was his job to finish all the leftovers in the family.

"Well, you know what they say—you are what you eat!" Dad said, waggling his eyebrows. He took a big bite. "And I'm *bananas*!"

I rolled my eyes. "Sorry, but I'm not in the mood for dadisms right now. And even on a normal day, that's a serious groaner."

Dad finished off the banana in three bites. "Don't worry, kiddo," he said when he finished chewing. "I'm sure you'll be hungry later."

I wasn't sure I'd ever be hungry again, but I didn't argue. I just nodded.

"Another day in bed is what you need," Dad added.

"Oh no, I'm not staying home," I announced. "I have to get back to school.

If I miss another day, I'll be buried alive in homework!"

Mom scowled. She put her hand on my forehead.

"Well, you don't have a fever," she said. "In fact, you're awfully cool. Dr. Phranc said we shouldn't worry unless you had a high temperature."

"I probably just had a bit of food poisoning," I said, brushing away her hand. "I'm not going to get anyone else sick. And I feel fine now."

Mom stared me down for another second, but then sighed. "All right. But you go straight to the nurse's office if being back at school is too much."

I gave Mom a hug and then stumbled back up to my room. Less than an hour later I was showered, dressed, and heading out the door.

I was feeling great as I made my way to the bus stop. I was excited to finally be back among the living. But apparently somebody forgot to tell my face. Because Nikki shot me a weird look when I joined her at the stop.

"Are you OK?" she asked. Her eyebrows scrunched together as she squinted at me. "You're walking funny, and you look sort of . . . gray."

"Yes!" I insisted. "I'm feeling so much better!"

Nikki gave me another look out of the corners of her eyes. "OK, Tulah. But you better not get sick again before auditions tomorrow."

"Did you have to bring auditions up?" I asked with a groan. "I'll be there, no matter what."

Nikki held up her little finger. "Pinky swear?" she asked.

I hooked my finger with hers. "Pinky swear," I said.

I waited for my stomach to start doing flips at the mention of my doom. Nothing happened. Maybe it was just too tired after the acrobatics of the last four days.

The bus arrived a few minutes later. Nikki leaped up the steps like she had springs in her sneakers. I followed behind.

I wasn't bouncing, but somehow I totally missed the last step.

THUNK!

I sprawled facedown in the aisle, and the bus erupted in giggles and snorts.

Great. Everyone had a front-row seat to my humiliation.

"Enjoy the show," I muttered.

"Are you OK?" Nikki asked as she bent down next to me.

"Yeah," I started. "I'm—"

But a slow *CLAP, CLAP, CLAP* interrupted my reply. I looked up and wished I could sink all the way into the grimy floor. My nemesis, Bella Gulosi, was smirking and giving me a hand—but not the helpful kind.

"Wow, Tulah. I thought a cross-country runner like you would be a little more graceful on her feet," Bella said. Her grin grew wider. "Or maybe you're just getting ready to 'break a leg' at auditions? Isn't it a little early for you to go stealing the spotlight?"

"Wow. You're *sooo* funny, Bella!" Nikki shot back. "Too bad we're not doing a comedy, or you'd be the star for sure!"

Nikki lifted me up by my elbow, and I dusted off my knees.

"Well, at least nothing seems to be bruised except my pride," I joked. But the sting of shame got worse when I looked down the aisle.

At the very back of the bus sat Jeremy Romero. He was the new boy whose name I had written a hundred times on the inside cover of my history notebook. Not that I was obsessed or anything.

Of course my crush would notice me at my absolute most embarrassing moment! He was staring right at me with those liquid chocolate eyes.

I quickly looked away. My cheeks burned. My knees started to weaken.

Nikki pulled me into a seat before I went down again. "Don't freak out on me, Tulah!" she whispered.

Nikki knew my reaction to crushes was a lot like my reaction to performing onstage. I tended to freeze up and stammer. I even forgot simple things like my name and how to speak in complete sentences. Just being in the same room (or bus) as Jeremy Romero made my mind go mushy.

"Breathe," Nikki whispered. "And try not to think about him. We'll deal with your love life *after* we tackle auditions."

At school the first three periods went by in a blur, but they all had one thing in common. Each teacher gave me the same furrowed-eyebrow look of concern and asked if I was OK. In the halls it wasn't much better.

"Yikes, Tulah. You look like you've been raised from the dead," Lacey said when she caught up to me before lunch. She was always blunt. "I'm kind of afraid to eat the cafeteria food now!"

"Here." I handed her the bag lunch Dad had packed. I still didn't feel like eating. "I can't even go in there. Too many bad memories. Tell Nikki I'm going to the library, OK?"

Lacey nodded absently. She was already digging through my lunch. I spun around to head toward the library.

It was a mistake. My stiff legs couldn't handle the sudden change in direction.

"*EEP!*" I yelped, but Lacey grabbed my elbow before I face-planted on the floor.

"Whoa, do you need me to walk you there?" Lacey asked. "Or maybe you should see the nurse."

I brushed her off. "I'm fine!" I insisted.

By focusing on my feet, I managed to stay (mostly) upright for the rest of the day. But everyone's worried looks were getting seriously annoying.

So after the last bell sounded, I got on the bus and went straight home. I had a ton of homework, and I was looking forward to being someplace where people just treated me normally.

When I pushed open the front door, though, something was already weird. King Kong, our dog, was not there to greet me.

"King! Here, big guy!" I called.

Usually he waited right inside, wagging his little French bulldog tail off. But the entry was empty.

"Wow. You look awful," Jaybee said when I stepped into the kitchen.

"Gee, thanks," I muttered. At least my brother was treating me normally.

I dropped my bag and went over to the counter. Jaybee was busy making his after-school snack of three PB&J sandwiches. Maybe King was nearby, hoping he could catch some peanut butter drippings. It would *almost* explain his lack of greeting.

I peeked around the counter. King was right there. When I stepped closer, he jumped up.

RRRRRRARF!

I stared. My furry friend had barked at me like I was a stranger!

"What's up, Big K?" I asked. "Did I scare you? Were you too focused on cleaning peanut butter off the floor?"

"Or he was just shocked by your face," Jaybee joked.

I glared at my dumb brother and then squatted down and waited for King to come wiggle all over me. But he approached slowly—like he was nervous. Then he began sniffing me cautiously.

"Hey, don't you recognize me?" I said, half laughing.

I thought dogs were supposed to be loyal. But one round of food poisoning, and King Kong was acting like we'd never met! After a final sniff, he turned and waddled out of the kitchen. While food was being prepared. That was definitely not like him.

Jaybee watched King leave and turned back to me. He squinted at my face.

"You OK?" he asked. "You seem . . . different."

"Yes!" I said, rolling my eyes. "I'm OK. Why does everyone keep asking me that?"

It wasn't like Jaybee to care if I was OK or not. I mean, he was your typical little brother—annoying. He only cared about his comics, old horror movies, and our dog, King Kong. In fact, King was the one thing we agreed on. (Because King Kong was, without a doubt, the cutest and best dog in the whole world.)

"Wait, that's it!" I suddenly yelled.

Jaybee jumped and slopped jam all over the counter. "That's *what*?" he asked as he licked the sticky fruit gunk off his thumb.

"That's why King is being weird. Today is September 27. It's his birthday!" I exclaimed. "I can't believe I forgot."

Most dogs don't get birthday parties, but in the Jones house we liked to celebrate our pooch. On the special day, he always got a little extra food, extra pets, a present, and a steak of his very own.

I was in such a hurry to get back to school this morning, I hadn't given King his birthday belly rub! I hadn't even said good morning.

"King!" I called, expecting him to come bounding back.

But he slowly walked in with his big ears standing straight up. Then he plopped down in the middle of the kitchen. He was more upset than I thought.

"I'm sorry, buddy. Are you mad because I forgot your birthday?" I asked.

His tail didn't even wag.

Luckily I knew how to make it up to him. I walked over to the fridge.

"Tulah," Jaybee said, eyeing me suspiciously. "What are you doing?"

"I know, I know. Mom might not be too thrilled with me for starting the party without her," I said, opening the fridge. "But I have to do what I have to do. I have to get King back on my side."

Time for your present, King!

Mom always went all out for our dog. King's steak was grass-fed, organic beef.
Usually raw meat totally grossed me out. But this . . .

!!
!!!
?!
. . . was DELICIOUS!

"Tulah, you're still not hungry?" Dad asked that night at the dinner table.

I shook my head and shot a glare at Jaybee. But my brother wasn't even looking at me. He was staring at his macaroni and cheese as if it were the most interesting thing in the world.

I got why he couldn't look at me. He'd seen me eat a huge, raw steak with my bare hands only a few hours ago. He must be totally grossed out. *I* was totally grossed out. When I realized what I'd done, I had rushed to my room, shut the door, and stayed there until Mom made me come out for supper.

"I had a big snack after school," I explained to Dad. It wasn't a lie. "My appetite isn't exactly what it used to be."

Jaybee coughed into his napkin. It sounded suspiciously like he said, "I'll say."

But when I glared at him again, he was focused back on his cheesy noodles.

I crossed my fingers under the table. *Please, please, please keep your mouth shut, Jaybee,* I silently pleaded.

The steak thing was more than weird. I mean, who chows down on raw meat like that? Definitely not me—the vegetarian. Especially because I couldn't even put a piece of fruit in my mouth that morning.

But when I had unwrapped King's steak, this weird, overwhelming urge came over me. I had to have the meat. I had to eat it RIGHT THEN and RIGHT THERE. I didn't have a choice.

I drooled a little just thinking about it. I quickly wiped it away with my napkin.

Maybe my body really needed the protein, I reasoned in my head. I'd been without food for a while, after all. That *had* to be the explanation for my sudden craving.

Right? Right!

But way deep down, I wasn't so sure. I stared down at my plate. For the first time ever I didn't even want a bite of my dad's famous macaroni and cheese. It looked like slimy maggots.

I pushed the disgusting mass of food around as dinner dragged on. I had to make it look like I was eating *something.* When nobody was watching, I flicked a few noodles onto the floor for King.

He slurped up the scraps, but my dog still wasn't happy. He made that very clear by keeping his back to me. It was going to take more than mac 'n' cheese bits to make up for gobbling his birthday steak.

When everyone else had finished, I bolted from the table. I just wanted to be alone.

"Hold on, Tulah," Mom said. "Aren't you forgetting something?"

I froze and looked down at my plate of untouched food. She wasn't going to make me eat it, was she? The thought made me want to hurl.

I frowned. "I'm really not hungry, Mom."

"I mean King's birthday!" she said, smiling. "It's time for his steak!"

I frowned deeper. "I, um . . ."

"We already gave him his steak," Jaybee said, real casual. I whipped my head around to stare at my brother.

Mom looked disappointed. "You did?"

"Yeah, you should've seen him tear into that thing!" Jaybee said, grinning and shaking his head. "He loved it."

Dad reached down and ruffled King's head. "Happy birthday, King Kong. You still look like a pup!"

Jaybee got out the new squeaky toy we'd wrapped up for him and dropped it in front of King. We all watched him shred the paper and strut around with his new prize. Then that was that.

I breathed a tiny sigh of relief. I couldn't believe Mom wasn't upset about the steak, or that Jaybee had covered for me. I had no idea why he'd do that, but I wasn't about to stick around to ask him.

"I gotta go finish my homework," I said, then shot up the stairs without waiting for a reply.

I felt my phone buzz in my pocket before I even got to my room. It had been buzzing since the end of school. Nikki had been trying to reach me, and I had been trying not to notice.

It was time to face the music.

"Stop ignoring me!" Nikki said as soon as I answered the call. Her face scowled at me through the screen. "I know *you* don't want to land a part in *Musical High*, but you swore you would do this. I'm counting on you! You know I'm dying to play Poodle! She's the comedic role of a lifetime!"

"I know, I know," I moaned into the phone.

In *Musical High*, Poodle was the drama co-president—and the perfect role for Nikki. Poodle was kind of the villain in the story, but she was also silly and sassy and had tons of funny lines.

For auditions we had been working on a duet between Poodle and her twin sister, Rayna. I was singing Rayna's part. It was a really fun, upbeat song. I had to admit we sounded pretty good.

"Don't worry. I'm not backing out," I told Nikki. "I just can't promise how great I'll be tomorrow."

"You'll be fine, Tulah," Nikki said. "In fact, I think you'd be great as Isabella."

"Ha!" I laughed. "*Me* play the lead? I doubt they'd even cast me in the chorus, since I can't stay upright onstage."

"You *will* be fine," Nikki said again. "Now, come on. Enough whining. It's time for practice!"

We ran through the song a few times. Our harmony was spot on.
But I always sounded great in my bedroom.

And Nikki had probably never been nervous in her life!

That was so awesome! Just sing like that onstage, and we're set.

"Yeah, sure. No problem," I said, trying not to sound too sarcastic. Performing onstage like I did in the privacy of my own bedroom was *exactly* the problem.

"Oh, and one more thing," Nikki added. "I know you're nervous, but try to get some sleep. Tomorrow is the big day, and you look exhausted. I need you healthy and ready to sing!"

As soon as I ended the call, I checked my face in the mirror. I *did* look super tired, but I didn't feel it. At all. In spite of the dark circles, my eyes felt like they were glued open and might never shut again.

Maybe it was stage fright jitters? Or possibly the two days of sleep I'd gotten recently. Whatever it was, my wide-awake state was extremely helpful for tackling my math homework (which was usually a snore). I sped through three days' worth of equations and word problems.

"Done!" I shouted as I slammed my algebra book shut.

It felt great to be catching up so quickly, but that was enough homework for one night. If I didn't start chilling out soon, there was no way I was going to be able to fall asleep.

And Nikki was right. I needed all the rest I could get before auditions. There was already a strong chance I'd faint onstage from nerves. I couldn't risk falling over from sleepiness too!

So I put away the stacks of history and biology worksheets. I changed into pajamas and wandered down into the living room. Jaybee and King were sprawled on the couch watching TV. Monster Movie Classics was playing, of course.

"Perfect," I whispered.

Usually I didn't want anything to do with scary stuff. I could go to the basement, where Mom and Dad were probably watching something better. But Jaybee's movie choice might just be the thing to bore me to sleep.

I flopped down onto the couch. Jaybee raised an eyebrow, but he didn't say anything.

Apparently he was giving me the silent treatment. That was fine with me. I ignored him and focused on the screen.

The people in the movie shrieked so loud I thought the windows would shatter. They were fleeing in terror as a hulking monster guy stumbled through town.

"Wow, so original," I mumbled.

I didn't get why Jaybee was so into old horror movies. To me they all looked the same. Just a bunch of people running around and screaming.

But as I sat there, I got drawn in. I leaned forward and stared. A creepy feeling came over me. It started at the very tips of my toes and traveled up my whole body.

This time I wasn't
bored or disgusted.

I started to feel bad
for the monster.

Was my audition going to make
people run screaming too?

Or would they laugh? Or maybe they'd just feel embarrassed for me as I froze up and made a complete fool of myself.

I hugged the couch cushion tight, trying not to let out a scream of my own. I had no idea how *my* horror story was going to end, and the suspense was killing me.

CHAPTER 6

Things were looking seriously grim.

"Leave me alone!" the monster cried.

He was struggling to hold the doors to his home shut as the angry mob rammed against them. The townspeople burst through. They raised their flaming torches and jabbed their sharp pitchforks and . . .

"Bedtime!" Mom said as she came into the living room.

"But, Mom, I'm not even tired, and we gotta see how it ends!" Jaybee whined.

"You heard me, Jaybee. It's bedtime, for the both of you. Plus, whining is a sign of tiredness." Mom winked and added, "I rest my case."

There was no point in arguing with a lawyer. So Jaybee clicked off the TV, and I pulled myself off the couch. Besides, I didn't need to watch the movie to know how it would turn out. There was never a happy ending in store for the monster.

I trudged back to my room. But as I flopped onto my bed, I felt even further away from sleep than I had before the movie. I got up and paced in front of my bookshelf.

Read it. Read it. Read it twice, I thought as I scanned the shelves.

"Nothing to distract me here," I mumbled.

I tiptoed to Jaybee's room, still thinking about that stupid movie. I cracked the door open.

King Kong was curled up on the bed with Jaybee. Some nights King slept on my bed, but I wasn't going to push him. Not after stealing his birthday steak. He did at least wag his tail when he saw me. I think he was starting to come around.

"Hey, Jay," I whispered. "Can I borrow a few of your *Zombie Boy Z* comics?"

Jaybee gave me a look, like the one he'd given me when I scarfed down raw flesh a few hours ago. Like he couldn't believe his eyes. Or in this case, his ears.

"Since when do you care about *Zombie Boy Z*? *My* favorite comic?" he hissed back. "And why were you watching Monster Movie Classics tonight? What's up with you, Tulah?"

I crossed my arms. "Not that it's any of your business, but I can't sleep. Your dumb horror stuff usually sends me straight to snoozeville."

What I didn't tell him was that the old horror movie was still haunting me. I couldn't stop thinking about the monster. How did he feel? Did he want to be a monster? Did he have any friends? I was weirdly craving another ghoulish story.

Jaybee didn't look convinced. He just scrunched his eyebrows and continued to stare.

"I have auditions tomorrow. You know how nervous I get," I added. "I need a distraction."

Jaybee shot me a final look before sliding out of bed. He grabbed a stack of comics off the floor and handed them over.

"Make sure you start with the first one," he said softly.

Back in bed, I began leafing through my brother's ridiculous comics. *Zombie Boy Z* was the tale of one reanimated boy's adventures after a horrible undead disease swept the world. Boy Z just wanted to live in peace, but the surviving humans kept hunting him down.

At first I laughed at the silly story, but soon I became quiet as I got sucked into Boy Z's journey. I sped through the first issue. Then the next. And the next. I was just about to start issue sixty-eight when a ray of sun broke through the crack in my curtains.

I blinked against the bright light. It was morning! I'd been reading all night.

I set down the comic, and my hand hit something wet.

"Ew," I gasped. "What . . ."

I followed a damp trail up my blanket all the way to my chin. "Drooling? I'm seriously drooling?" I wondered out loud.

I wiped the saliva and did my best to dry my hand on my soaked blanket. Since when did I forget to close my mouth while I read?

I shut my eyes. *It's nerves,* I told myself. *You're nervous about the audition today. It's making you forget things. That's all.*

But another voice was shouting from some deep, dark cellar in my brain. *REALLY? How do you forget to keep spit inside your mouth? Or sleep? Those aren't things you just forget. This is not stage fright, and you know it!*

I shoved those thoughts away and threw Jaybee's comic onto the floor. What I needed to do was just get up and get ready for the day.

But I could barely get my legs to move.

My arms were stiff too. It was like my mind was awake, but my body was out cold!

When I looked in the mirror, I almost screamed. I definitely could've used some beauty sleep!
I did what I could with Mom's makeup. But I hadn't had much practice.

I carefully made my way down the stairs for breakfast. "My appetite has to be regular by now," I said to myself. "Right?"

Wrong. The bowl of oatmeal Dad left for me on the table looked disgusting. (More disgusting than oatmeal usually looked.) I couldn't bring myself to touch it.

"Sweetie! You must be so nervous about the audition!" Mom said when she came into the kitchen. She saw me staring down at the bowl of lumpy beige gunk.

"Yeah, that must be it," I said. I looked up and Mom gasped.

"Oh! Did you get into my makeup? Is that for auditions? You know, you should really ask. And maybe tone it down a bit." She started rubbing at my face with a napkin.

Jaybee was wolfing down his oatmeal (which was smothered in brown sugar and butter) and trying not to laugh.

I let out a big sigh. "I can't wait until today is over."

"You'll be amazing. Don't let the jitters get to you," Mom said, taking one last swipe at my clown face.

"I'll try not to," I mumbled as Mom went to the counter to make her coffee.

But that was when I realized—I wasn't feeling *any* of my usual jitters. I looked down at my hands. They weren't shaky or sweaty. Butterflies weren't flapping in my stomach. I only felt that uneasy fear back in the deep, dark cellar of my mind.

I put my hand over my heart. It had to be thumping out of control, just like always.

I moved my hand farther left. Then right.

My heart was definitely not thumping out of control.

In fact . . . my heart wasn't beating at all!

"Tulah," Jaybee said from across the table. He put down his spoon. "Are you OK? Really?"

"Just nerves," I managed to gasp.

I hoped he was convinced. I didn't know if I was.

Get a grip, Tulah, I told myself as I stood up from the table. *If your heart wasn't beating, you'd be DEAD . . . or a zombie . . . and that is IMPOSSIBLE.*

I shoved that thought back into the dark cellar of my brain as I scraped my bowl of uneaten mush into the garbage. I kept my back to Mom so she wouldn't see.

I am not dead, I told myself. *I'm as alive as the rest of my family! We're all just living normal lives, eating our normal breakfast (well . . . attempting to eat), and getting ready for a normal day. You've just been reading too many zombie comics!*

It was clear. Too many comics plus one upcoming audition added to Crazy Tulah. That had to be it. It had to be!

I stumbled up the stairs and into my room to grab my backpack. Jaybee was already there, gathering up his comics. They were still scattered around my bed. When he saw me, he straightened up and took a deep breath.

"Tulah, listen," he started to say. "You—"

"Not now!" I groaned.

It looked like Jaybee was about to launch into a big geek speech, but I was not in the mood for a lecture about respecting a comic's collector value or whatever.

He gave me a weird look. Then he carefully ripped a page from the *Zombie Boy Z* he was holding. Since when did Jaybee damage his comics?

He held out the page. "Just take this."

"Fine. Whatever." I said, grabbing it.

I glanced at the page—some zombie apocalypse quiz—and shoved it into my pocket. I did not have time for any nerd business.

One of Dad's corny mottos played in my head as I stumbled down the stairs and out the door. "Sometimes the only way out is through," he liked to say. Right now I was taking that dadism to heart. Somehow I just had to get through this day!

Nikki was waiting at the bus stop, just like normal. *Normal. Normal. Normal.* I said the word in my head, hoping if I repeated it enough it would make it true. *It's a normal day. Everything is normal. I am normal.*

"Oh, you poor thing!" Nikki gasped when she saw me.

"What?" I put my hand on my face. I thought Mom had fixed my makeup disaster.

"You look so . . . nervous!" Nikki replied. "Calm down! The audition is no big deal. It'll be over before you know it."

I forced a smile. Right. It was *normal* to be nervous. "Sorry, I-I'm just worried that I'll blow this audition. For you, I mean," I stammered.

"Don't worry!" Nikki grabbed my arm and took me up the bus steps. "We're going to knock 'em dead."

I nodded. But for some reason that didn't make me feel any better.

When we got school, Nikki skipped down the bus steps. She was clearly *very* excited for auditions.

"Hurry up," she called over her shoulder.

I was moving slowly, like a girl who hadn't slept all night and had only eaten a single slab of beef in five days. By the time I got to my locker, Nikki was slamming hers shut.

"Pick it up, Tulah! History will be history by the time we get there!"

I slid into my seat just as the bell rang. Ms. Perez was a stickler for tardiness, and always started right on time.

"Can someone get the lights?" Ms. Perez asked. She had her PowerPoint presentation all set up. She hit her clicker and the first slide appeared on screen.

The title was in big, black letters. Below it was the subtitle, "Plague in Medieval Times." And below *that* was a painting of a pile of dead bodies.

"*Ugh.*" The groan quietly escaped my mouth. I crossed my arms on my desk and put my head down. I could not think about death right now.

I was so focused on *not* focusing, I must've drowned everything else out. Because when the lights came back on and I lifted my head, something shiny gleamed on my desk. It was a puddle of drool!

I quickly wiped up the mini lake with my sleeve, but not before the kid next to me got a look at it. He snickered.

"I guess I fell asleep," I mumbled.

I was careful to keep my head up and my mouth closed for the rest of my classes. At lunch I told Nikki that I was going to the library again.

"Still can't return to the scene of the crime, huh?" she teased.

"No, not yet. Plus, I have homework to make up," I lied. I'd made good progress last night, but I just needed an excuse to go anywhere but the dreaded cafeteria.

"Guess I'll have to risk it alone!" Nikki said with a wave.

Soon the last period arrived—biology.

My lab partner was easy to pick out under the fluorescent lights. Angela Stone was the dark spot in a sea of color. She dressed in black (always) and tended to lurk in corners.

Maybe Angela's spooky look was due to the fact that her family owned the only funeral home in town (so it was convenient for her to be dressed as a mourner at all times). Or maybe she simply hated color.

"Hi!" I said when I got to our table, trying to keep up my usually cheery mood.

Angela nodded silently, and then went back to reading her book.

I plopped into my seat. A lot of kids thought Angela was weird. Even I had to admit she was unique, but I'd worked with her backstage on a couple of school plays. While she wasn't a talker, and her attraction to dark corners was odd, she was honestly harmless.

"Good afternoon, class!" Ms. Rogi said at the front of the room. "Are you ready? It's the big one today. We'll be dissecting frogs!"

"Just great," I muttered. I'd been focusing so hard on being normal that I'd completely forgotten we had a dissection today.

As part of our anatomy unit, we had already sliced and diced an earthworm and a chicken wing. And by "we," I meant Angela.

When we were first partnered, I had told Angela I had trouble with cutting up animals because I was a vegetarian. (Which was true . . . until yesterday!) She had simply nodded and pretended not to notice that I never took a turn with the scalpel.

Angela might be odd, but she was the perfect lab partner—smart, quiet, and not at all squeamish. She did *all* the gross stuff without flinching.

Ms. Rogi started passing out dissection pans. "Please put on your gloves and goggles," she told the class.

I snapped on my gloves (even though I had no plans of touching a dead frog) and picked up a clipboard and pencil. As always, I was ready to take notes while Angela did the cutting.

Ms. Rogi set a tray on our table. The frog was already lying belly down in it. His arms and legs stuck out stiffly.

A sour, pickle-like odor suddenly hit my nose.

I drew back. "*Ugh*, what's that smell?" I asked Angela.

"Formaldehyde," she answered.

Angela didn't even blink at the stench. "Stinks, huh? You get used to it. It keeps the corpse from rotting."

Um. *Ewww!*

On a *normal* day I would've been fighting my gag reflex hard. But I guess I was too distracted by auditions to be bothered. I reached out and jiggled one of the frog's webbed feet. His legs didn't bend at all. He just rocked back and forth. He was stiffer than I was!

"Poor guy. Why is he so rigid?" I asked.

"Formaldehyde doesn't keep the *rigor mortis* from settling in," Angela explained. "*Rigor mortis* is the process of muscles getting super stiff when something dies."

I jiggled Mr. Frog again, fascinated. But then I noticed Angela's puzzled look. I made a grossed-out face and yanked my hand back.

Act normal, I reminded myself. Normal me would want nothing to do with a dead thing.

All I had to do was keep up my normal act through this class and auditions. Then, after my weird stage fright nerves were out of my system, things would get back to *real* normal.

"OK, let's do this," I whispered to myself.

I started to read down the list of things we needed to observe. First we noted the size of the muscles in the arms and legs. Next we had to observe the skin by touching it.

"Don't worry. I can do that part," Angela said. She never had a problem with slime, where as I could not handle anything remotely sticky.

But I suddenly found myself reaching out to touch the dead thing, *again*. Like it was no big whoop. Angela looked at my hand and then back at me.

"Yep. It feels slimy and wet and kind of squishy," I said casually, noting it on our paper.

"Yeah . . . that's because of the special type of skin frogs have. They're able to take in oxygen through it," Angela explained. She was still staring at me. "Hey, are you feeling OK?"

I nodded. I was OK. Really OK. Despite the frog corpse splayed out in front of me, I wasn't grossed out. It was kind of nice not having the urge to run away screaming.

I flipped Kermit over. We had reached the end of our external observations. Next up were the internal ones. It was time to start cutting.

Angela picked up the special dissection scissors. We had to make cuts to open the frog's mouth wider. She snipped one side, and suddenly I knew I could do the other without passing out.

"Oh, I got it!" I said and reached right for the scissors.

Angela gasped and covered her mouth. What, now she was the woozy one?

Oh my gosh, Tulah, are you OK?
I told you, I'm . . .

. . . fine!

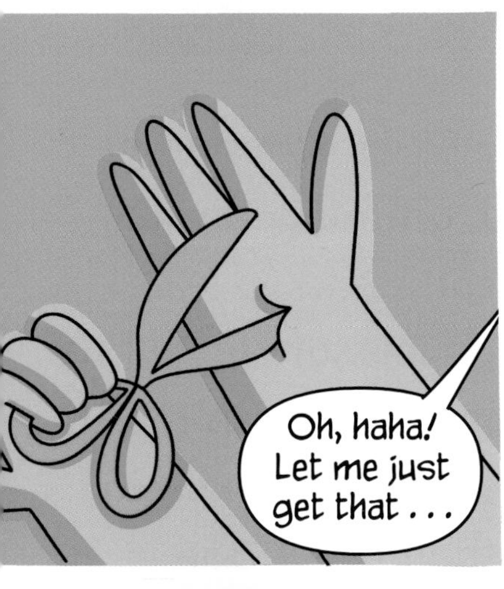
Oh, haha! Let me just get that . . .

I got it!
AH!

Heh. Clumsy me. Heh.

"S-sorry about that!" I stammered. "At least the frog's fine. I mean, besides being dead. I'm not usually this clumsy, but I didn't get much sleep last night. Because of auditions today. You heard about auditions, right? Well, long story but I'm trying out and I get so nervous and—" I started babbling and couldn't stop. Angela just stared.

"Don't worry. A couple of scratches never killed anyone," I finished, grinning like an idiot. "I'm fine. No big deal!"

Honestly, I was trying to reassure myself as much as my lab partner. But I wasn't sure it was working. On either of us. Angela had gotten even quieter than usual. She looked . . . concerned.

"I'm fine." I repeated.

Fine, Fine. Fine, I screamed in my head. *Accidents happen. Perfectly normal.*

Except cuts usually hurt, or at least stung. And these hadn't hurt a bit.

The rest of biology was awkward, to say the least. Luckily no one had noticed my accident, except Angela.

My dark cloud of a lab partner stared as I put an extra lab glove over my injured hand. She leaned closer, looking at the cut on my face.

"Huh. You're not bleeding," Angela said.

I quickly slapped my good hand over the wound. "Only a little," I lied. I smiled big. "Nothing to worry about. Come on, we have to finish the dissection."

After a long minute of more staring, Angela nodded and picked up the scissors. I let out a small sigh of relief as she went back to snipping the frog.

While Angela made the cuts, I sneaked a look at my cheek in the shiny metal of our scalpel. Angela was right. There wasn't a single drop of blood. And not a single spark of pain. That was definitely *not* normal.

When the bell rang, I sprang to my feet.

"Tulah, do you want me to—" I heard Angela calling after me. But I kept going. I didn't want her to do anything!

I hustled on stiff legs through the hallways, feeling as rigid as the frog we'd just sliced. Everywhere kids were buzzing about auditions.

"Only fifteen minutes!" someone yelled.

"Do you have any lip gloss?" a girl asked.

I stumbled past the crowd and into the girls' room. I went straight into the first open stall, closed the door, and leaned against it. My phone vibrated in my pocket. I ignored it.

Instead I unclenched my fist to check the damage. *Yep.* I had a pretty big gash. I touched my face and felt the dry cut.

I dug out a Band-Aid from my backpack and slapped it onto my face. I didn't technically need a Band-Aid since I wasn't bleeding, but I just wanted something to cover my weird wound.

As I leaned against the stall door, rapid-fire thoughts bounced around in my head. I had two deep cuts, but they didn't hurt and I wasn't bleeding. There was no way I could convince myself this was normal—or the result of stage fright. But I also couldn't allow myself to think about what my creepy symptoms might mean.

I tried to duck my flying thoughts like I was playing a game of mental dodgeball. Then one thought hit me right in the stomach.

Living people bleed. Dead people don't.

NO! *Nerves. Nerves. Nerves. Normal. Normal. Normal,* I repeated in my head, trying to shake it all off.

Suddenly the bathroom door banged open. A familiar voice spoke. "Tulah?"

It was Nikki.

"You can't hide from this, Tulah!" she said loudly.

If she only knew.

Nikki's hand appeared under the stall. She held out her pinky. "It's time," she said, wiggling her little finger to remind me of my promise.

I let out a deep sigh. Then I made sure my Band-Aid was on tight, shoved my injured hand into my pocked, and came out of my bathroom cell. For the past two weeks I'd been worried about this audition. About messing up. About letting Nikki down. But something had changed.

I was still worried. Don't get me wrong. But I wasn't freaked out about the audience. I was freaked out because I was starting to feel . . . like . . . like a *freak*!

I was about to be on display for the whole world (or at least a whole auditorium of kids) to see.

"I don't know if I can do this, Nikki. What if I mess up?" I asked. Maybe she'd take pity on me and let me off the hook.

"You won't," Nikki answered. She took out strawberry lip gloss and put some on in front of the mirror. "You've practiced so much, Tulah. You've got this."

"What if I fall on my face and hit my head and get a concussion? That could happen," I argued.

"Looks like you already did, so you don't have to worry!" She pointed at the covered up cut on my face. "What's up with the Band-Aid, anyway?"

"Dissection accident in biology," I said. "But seriously, Nikki. What if I can't even speak?"

"Then focus on singing," she replied.

I was getting desperate. "What if I—"

Nikki held up a hand. "What if we go get this over with?" she suggested, smiling.

I was out of arguments.

It was time to meet my fate.
YOU'RE THE ATEMS
AUDITION TODAY
The only thing worse than auditioning was auditioning in front of EVERYONE!

Some of the kids (like my Jeremy, obviously) were really great . . .

Others, not so much.

"Up next," Mr. Hammer said from his table, "Nikki Corvos and Tulah Jones."

I couldn't move. I felt completely numb.

"Come on, Tulah," Nikki whispered as she pulled me out of my seat. "Just get it over with."

She dragged me along, and I bumbled my way up the steps. My stiff legs were protesting as much as I was. I couldn't believe I was really doing this. Everyone was about to see what a freak I was.

Onstage the lights were so bright I couldn't see anyone in the auditorium.

"See, it's like we're all alone!" Nikki said.

I gave a stiff nod, and Nikki gave our music to the piano accompanist.

I stood in the spotlight and waited for the panic. The freeze. The sweat . . .

But the feelings never came. My stomach wasn't churning. My hands weren't sweating. My heart wasn't pounding.

The music began. I opened my mouth to sing, and that's when the miracle happened.

Instead of panicking about being onstage (or feeling nervous about my weird changes), I just felt . . .
AMAZING!

Normal Tulah would've been lying facedown on the stage by now, but the all-new Tulah? She didn't have guts that twisted and squirmed and made her panic. This Tulah could just relax and really *sing*!

When I realized I wasn't going to make a total fool of myself, I let go even more. I belted out my last solo verse with all my heart. From the corner of my eye, I caught a glimpse of Nikki. She looked a little surprised and a lot impressed.

We got through the song without missing a single beat. It was just like we'd practiced—only a million times better! When the music finished, I heard cheers. The spotlights went down, and I saw Jeremy Romero standing up in the audience, clapping.

Nikki hugged me. "I knew you could do it!" she whispered. "That was awesome!"

I felt like my feet didn't hit the floor as we walked offstage. I was so happy that I didn't even care about my painless cuts, or turning carnivore, or not being able to sleep, or what any of it meant. If whatever was going on allowed me to do what I loved—I'd take it!

Broadway here I come!

I was picturing my name in lights when Mr. Hammer started speaking. "If I call your name, please come to the stage," he said. "Clay Sanderson, Becka Hayes, Jeremy Romero, Nikki Corvos, Tulah Jones . . ."

Mr. Hammer kept listing names as Nikki and I went to the front of the auditorium. My musical dreams were coming true! I felt focused, excited, overjoyed—things I'd NEVER felt before on a stage.

I peered down the row of kids. Maybe we

would sing the closing number together?

I couldn't wait. This was the best day ever.

Until Mr. Hammer made the announcement.

"Ms. Raimi is going to teach you all some simple dance steps and see how you move!" he said.

Every bit of good feeling drained out of me so fast I was worried that people would see it like a puddle on the floor.

Before Monday, doing a dance number wouldn't have sounded so bad. Old Tulah could dance. Old Tulah had moves. New Tulah's moves were more like Frankenstein's. They usually ended with me on the floor—or stabbing myself with scissors. And that was just when I was trying to walk around and do regular stuff.

But dancing? With a group? Someone could end up hospitalized!

I turned to Nikki and whispered, "I'm so dead."

Ms. Raimi, the dance teacher, nodded to the piano player. An upbeat song filled the auditorium. We watched as Ms. Raimi ran through the dance steps. It didn't *look* hard. But then again, neither had climbing the bus stairs, and we all know how that turned out.

"OK, let's take it half time!" Ms. Raimi called out. "All together! Kick. Step. Touch. Left! Move. Move. Move."

I tried my best to keep up with the dance, but my legs were rigid. *At least you're still standing,* I told myself.

"Now let's add the arms!" Ms. Raimi chirped.

"Let's not," I mumbled.

Kick.
Step. Touch.
Left!

I was about as graceful as the Tin Man from *The Wizard of Oz*, before he gets his oil.

All together now!
EEK!

I'm all right!
I was definitely not all right.

I dragged myself backstage before anyone could get a good look. My right arm was dangling by my side like a piñata!

I tried to move it, but my arm didn't budge. I nudged it with my left pointer finger. The arm swung lifelessly back and forth.

I gulped. My arm looked like it had fallen off and then somebody stuck it on backward. It practically hurt to look at, but I wasn't feeling any pain.

It was just like the dissection accident. This definitely should've hurt. But it definitely didn't.

"Oh man, oh man, oh man," I whispered as stumbled into the costume shop. I managed to make it inside without dislocating anything else.

The voice in my head, the one I had been trying to keep quiet in the dark cellar of my mind, was screaming too loud to be ignored any longer:

THIS ISN'T NORMAL, TULAH JONES!!!

I suddenly felt something crinkle in my back pocket. I reached in and took out a piece of paper.

It was the page from *Zombie Boy Z* that Jaybee had given me that morning. I slowly unfolded it.

I stared at the paper. My brother had figured out something wasn't right too. He had tried to tell me.

I uncapped a pen and started to tick off boxes with my working hand.

My life was officially over.
I was . . . UNDEAD!

The writing was on the page. These were the facts.

1. Like Zombie Boy Z, I'd apparently eaten something rotten and gotten sick. (Thanks a lot, Mystery Meatless lunch.)

2. And like Zombie Boy Z, when I thought I'd been sleeping off a nasty bit of food poisoning, I'd actually been dying! I hadn't just woken up after being sick—I had been reanimated.

3. **OMG. OMG. OMG. I was a ZOMBIE.**

"*Noooooooooooo,*" I moaned.

I slapped my working hand over my mouth. I even sounded like a monster!

What should I do now? Ten minutes ago I was having the time of my life onstage—something I never thought would happen.

But now I'm dead, sort of—something I never thought would happen (or at least not in sixth grade)!

I lurched up and down the rows of costumes, racking my brain. I had no idea how to be dead! I had a hard enough time being alive.

This wasn't like one of Jaybee's movies either. This was real life, or undeath, or whatever. This was *my* undead life, and I could not let it become a nightmare! If anyone found out, I would be run out of town, buried, or experimented on. I could not let that happen.

Yes, I was dead, but I sure wasn't done living. I still wanted to go to school, hang out with my friends, pet my dog . . .

I stared at my zombie face in the mirror. "Nobody can know you're dead," I told myself. "Tulah, you've GOT to keep this a secret."

Then I screamed.

ANGELA?!?

You look like you saw a ghost. Or maybe I did?
How long have you been standing there?

Wait! What are you doing? Wh–

AAAH!

POP!
There!

I don't know what she did, but suddenly my arm was back in business!

"Wow!" I said, swinging it around.

"Wow," Angela echoed. "So, I guess you are dead."

"Uh, yeah," I said. "I kind of am."

There was no point in denying it after all she had seen and heard. I held my breath.

Luckily Angela didn't appear eager to drive a steak through my heart or lop off my head. Instead she looked at me the same way she looked at the dead frog in Ms. Rogi's class—like I was fascinating.

"Let me see your hand," she ordered.

I held out my wound, and she studied it. "I think we can do something with this," she said, more to herself than to me.

Angela dug around in her bag and took out a small tube of superglue. She squirted a glob into my wound and then pressed the skin together.

The gash was sealed.

"Mortician's trick," Angela explained matter-of-factly. She looked at my hand again and murmured, "So there wasn't any bleeding. Huh."

"Yeah. No beating heart, so no pumping blood," I said, tapping my chest.

"Of course," Angela said. "Which is why you look so washed out. . . ."

Angela sat me down in a chair at the makeup table. She pulled a few bottles and tubes out of her bag.

"I decided to gather a few supplies from home, after I witnessed your, uh, behavior in biology," she explained.

She held up a long strip of paper with a variety of skin tones next to my cheek. Then she took out a container. She started mixing up something that looked like the stuff Dad used to patch holes in walls.

"So . . . how come you're not freaking out?" I asked while she added color to the goop, getting just the right tone that matched my skin.

Angela shrugged. "I live in a funeral home. I see a lot of dead people. I'm pretty used to it. Dad is teaching me to do funeral makeup. Sometimes I even talk to the bodies while I work."

"You . . . talk . . . to bodies?" I repeated.

She slathered the cut on my face with the goo. Then she blended it until I could barely even tell the cut had been there at all. "Yeah, but you're the first one who's talked back."

"Speaking of talking, you won't tell anybody about me being—" I gestured to my face. "Will you? Because if anybody finds out . . ."

"Don't worry, dead girl," Angela said, snapping her bag shut. "As long as you don't start running around gnawing on people, your secret's safe with me."

I let out a sigh of relief and checked myself out in the mirror. I looked better than I had all week.

"Wow," I said. "Thanks so much, Angela. This is amazing."

Angela just gave a small smile and then helped me out of the makeup chair. I lurched over to the side door that led back to the auditorium seats.

Maybe, just maybe, I thought as I pushed through the door, *being dead is something I can live with after all.*

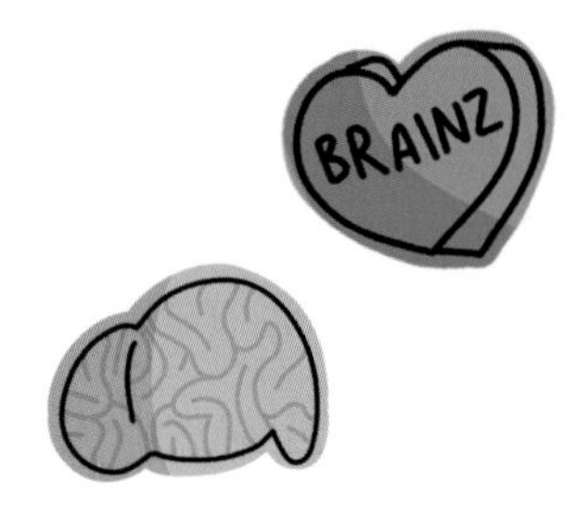

“Where have you been?” Nikki hissed. “Did you just *die*?”

I froze. I stared at my best friend. *How did she—?*

“And after you did so well during the singing portion! I guess you still have a few stage fright nerves to conquer,” she added.

I let out a shaky breath. Nikki wasn’t saying what I thought she was saying. She was talking about me dying from *embarrassment* over my dance performance. Not from some ghoulish zombie virus.

“I looked for you in the bathroom, but I didn’t see you,” Nikki continued. She looked me up and down. “Are you OK?”

After Angela's mini-makeover, I knew I looked better than I had in days. I nodded yes as I slid into my seat. I was afraid to open my mouth for fear of spilling my guts. It was beyond strange to keep a secret from Nikki. Especially a secret *this* strange!

But even though I wasn't a horror nerd like Jaybee, I knew what happened to undead creatures as soon as they were found out. Panic! Mayhem! Plus very unhappy endings for the monster. I didn't feel all that monstrous, but who knew how people would react if they found out I had no pulse?

I could not risk losing my best friend. That would be a fate worse than death.

"I was so mortified after my fall!" I managed to whisper. "I was hiding backstage while I recovered from the embarrassment."

Nikki gave me a hug, and we both turned back toward the front.

Mr. Hammer stood in the center of the stage and clapped his hands. "That's a wrap!" he called out. "You all did a wonderful job and have made our jobs very difficult. We'll be making decisions tonight and posting the cast list in the morning!"

I blew out a sigh of relief. At least I wouldn't need to repeat my bumbling dance performance. But my relief quickly turned into disappointment when I realized what that meant. I had totally blown it with my stage dive. My Broadway dreams were over just minutes after they were born. Even without the stage fright nerves, I'd still killed the possibility of performing.

That's fine, I thought as Nikki and I grabbed our things and filed out. *It would've been way too risky to be onstage anyway.* I also tried to remind myself that earlier today all I had wanted was for this to be over. That I never actually wanted a part. Now, it was over. At least for me.

My shoulder brushed the person next to me as I shuffled down the center aisle. I looked over to see Jeremy Romero walking next to me.

"Hey, Tulah. You were great up there." Jeremy smiled and then looked at his shoes.

"Thanks! So were you," I answered.

I ANSWERED! I actually talked to Jeremy Romero like, well, like a person! No stammering. No clamming up. No blushing.

I glanced over my shoulder at Nikki. She looked back at me with huge eyes, sending a silent *OMG*.

"So, see you here tomorrow?" Jeremy said when we got out into the hall.

Old Tulah would have been hightailing it for the hills, but new Tulah turned and looked right at Jeremy.

Our eyes met. If I didn't know any better, I'd swear my heart gave a thud.

"Definitely," I replied. "See you here bright and early!"

"I'll be looking for your name on that cast list," Jeremy added as he walked away toward his locker.

I crossed my fingers behind my back. I'd be looking for my name on that cast list too.

"Coming through!" Mr. Hammer said the next day.

He pushed his way through the pack of kids and taped a sheet of paper to the auditorium door. It was the cast list.

I tried to catch a glimpse from the back of the crowd, but Mr. Hammer stood right in front of the paper.

It had been agony waiting for this moment. Apparently being undead meant no more sleep. Ever. So I was up the whole night thinking about the musical, and my new zombified state.

I had a lot to figure out. Could I keep this a secret? How would I get food? Would I become a mindless monster? Jaybee had been over at a friend's house yesterday, so I couldn't ask him my questions. But this weekend I was going to corner him.

If anyone knew how to handle this, it was my brother, the zombie expert.

For now, though, I was focused on the musical. Mr. Hammer was making a speech about there being "no small parts" and how "everyone did an amazing job." But the mob of kids couldn't wait any longer. They pushed him out of the way.

Nikki reached the cast list first.

"Poodle! YES!" she shouted. "Oh, Tulah!" She pulled me closer. "Look!"

OMG

The words jumped out.

Isabella Montez .... Tulah Jones

I had been cast too! I was going to be onstage. As *Isabella*—the lead girl!

I squealed out loud. I couldn't believe it. Not after my dance disaster! But my eyes continued to scroll down.

I screamed when I saw the next name. Nikki laughed, and we both started jumping up and down.

Jeremy was going to play Todd Bolton!

Todd was the male lead, and the whole musical revolved around Isabella and Todd breaking down their school's cliques and stereotypes. Not to mention Isabella and Todd were totally in love! It was unreal that *I'd* be Jeremy's (stage) girlfriend.

I stopped screaming and stared down the hall. My leading man, in the flesh, was walking over.

Jeremy went right to the cast list and ran his finger down it. He paused on my name, and I thought I saw him smile. Then he slid his finger to his own name. He turned around and gave me the biggest smile I'd ever seen.

I couldn't help but smile back. I felt that thud in my chest, the same one I'd felt when we locked eyes. It was absolutely crazy. My life was literally over—but in some ways I felt like it was just beginning.

TULAH'S TERMS

corpse—simply put, a dead body

craving—wanting something in the worst way. Please, never let me crave human brains!

dislocate—to move a bone out of where it's supposed to connect to another bone. Dislocating something would probably hurt pretty bad if I was still alive.

dissection—when you cut something, like a frog, up into smaller parts and study it

flesh—the soft parts of a person or animal . . . like the parts I want to eat

food poisoning—to be blunt, throwing up and diarrhea caused by bacteria and other nasty stuff in food

formaldehyde—a gas that when dissolved in water makes the perfect mixture to stop most anything dead from rotting

funeral home—the place where dead people are prepared for burial or cremation. I wonder if they'd be able to help *undead* people too. . . .

lurch—to move with a jerky motion, and how zombies walk. I'm not going to win a dance contest anytime soon.

mortician—a person who prepares dead people for getting buried or cremated. Morticians make the best zombie stylists. (Thanks, Angela!)

mortified—beyond embarrassed

nemesis—the number-one enemy of your life. My nemesis, Bella Gulosi, is simply the worst.

numb—having no feeling or emotions. Zip. Zero. Zilch.

omnivore—a person or animal who eat plants (yuck) and animals (yum!)

reanimate—to bring back to life. I'm still trying to figure out how it worked for me!

rigid—super stiff and generally not bendy

scalpel—a small, thin-bladed knife that teachers give kids to cut up frogs (and that doctors use in surgery)

urge—a majorly strong desire that you can barely control

vegetarian—a person who doesn't eat meat. Hard to believe my raw-meat-loving self was ever satisfied with just vegetables, fruits, grains, nuts, eggs, and dairy.

zombie apocalypse—when a whole bunch of zombies rise up and attack all the living. It's worse than the middle school mean girls' rude attitudes at lunch, but just barely.

USE YOUR BRAAAINS!

Don't worry, I won't eat them.

1. Something seriously suspicious is going on behind those doors. Help me out and write what you think the cafeteria worker is doing. If you want, you could even write it like a story!

2. Living me would've been TERRIFIED to audition. Have you ever done something, even though you were nervous? What advice would you give to other kids who are about to face their fears (besides becoming a zombie who doesn't get butterflies in her stomach)?

3. Practice your mind-reading skills, and write what you think is going through my head in each of these panels. What makes you think that?

4. I was SO not expecting Angela to help me out. TBH, I thought she was going to end my undead life, not save it! Has someone ever helped you when you weren't expecting it? How did it feel?

5. Ugh. The moment I first ate raw meat. It was quite a shock. How does the art here help show how completely freaked out everyone is? (Try looking at the shape of the panels, the color in the background, people's expressions, and other tiny details.)

6. I had a hard time facing the truth about my new undead self. Did you figure out I was a zombie sooner? If you did, what made you think I had been reanimated? If you were as surprised as I was, look for clues in the story that hinted I was a member of the walking dead.

CRAVING MORE?
BRAINZ
I may be dead, but I've got a lot more living to do! Check out my other adventures.

OMG, ZOMBIE!

After eating a suspicious school meal, I feel different. REALLY different. Find out how my undead life began!

REALLY ROTTEN DRAMA

I'm dealing with a BFF crisis, my first-ever (stage) kiss, and my rotting zombie body! Can I put an end to this stinky situation?

TOTAL FREAK-OUT

No meat equals one grumpy zombie. Can I get enough food to keep my mood under control before the school dance?

GOT BRAINS?

I'm going on a retreat with the academic team (and my worst nemesis, Bella Gulosi!). Will I survive the weekend?

ABOUT THE AUTHOR

Emma T. Graves has authored more than ninety books for children and has written about characters both living and dead. When she's not writing, Emma enjoys watching classic horror movies, taking long walks in the nearby cemetery, and storing up food in her cellar. She is prepared for the zombie apocalypse.

ABOUT THE ILLUSTRATOR

Binny Boo, otherwise known as Ellie O'Shea, is a coffee addict, avid snowboarder, puppy fanatic—and an illustrator. Her love for art started at a young age. She spent her childhood drawing, watching cartoons, creating stories, and eating too many sweets for her own good. She graduated from Plymouth University in 2015 with a degree in illustration. She now lives in Worcester, UK, and feels so lucky that she gets to spend her days doing what she adores.